PIRATE PUG

The Dog Who Rocked the Boat

LAURA JAMES

Illustrated by ÉGLANTINE CEULEMANS

BLOOMSBURY
CHILDREN'S BOOKS
LONDON OXFORD NEW YORK NEW DELHI SYDNEY

BLOOMSBURY CHILDREN'S BOOKS
Bloomsbury Publishing Plc
50 Bedford Square, London WC1B 3DP, UK

BLOOMSBURY, BLOOMSBURY CHILDREN'S BOOKS and the Diana logo
are trademarks of Bloomsbury Publishing Plc

First published in Great Britain in 2019 by Bloomsbury Publishing Plc

A catalogue record for this book is available from the British Library

ISBN: PB: 978-1-4088-9594-8; eBook: 978-1-4088-9595-5

2 4 6 8 10 9 7 5 3

Typeset by Janene Spencer

Printed and bound in China by Leo Paper Products

**To find out more about our authors and books visit www.bloomsbury.com
and sign up for our newsletters**

For the Cary Gang

Finders Keepers' Island

N · **W** · **E** · **S**

Stub Toe Cove

Possible shark sighting

Rocks of Wrath

DANGER

Finders Keepers' Shack

Revenge Mountain

Cliffs of No Going Back

Creepy Lagoon

Surprisingly Big Trees

Pebbly Bay

BEWARE ALL YE WHO ENTER!

Chapter 1

It was no ordinary morning for Pug and his freckled companion, Lady Miranda. They weren't at home at No. 10, The Crescent. They were on holiday, staying in the best suite of the Smuggler's Rest Hotel, in the small town of Pebbly Bay.

Pug woke up feeling hungry, so he padded over to where Lady Miranda was sleeping and gave her a nudge, certain she'd want to know it was breakfast time.

Lady Miranda snorted and lifted her eye mask. She smiled at Pug, who wagged his tail.

There was a familiar knock on the bedroom door. Wendy, Lady Miranda's housekeeper, entered with the breakfast tray.

'Good morning, m'lady,' she said, placing the tray on Lady Miranda's

lap. 'I persuaded chef to make you some jam tarts.'

As Pug sniffed the tarts with delight, there was an unexpected *SQUAWK!* and a parrot flew into the room.

'Heavens!' exclaimed Wendy, flapping her arms above her head and running after it. 'How did that get in here?'

Lady Miranda fell about laughing as the parrot dodged Wendy and landed safely on the breakfast tray.

Pug guarded the jam tarts, but the parrot didn't seem interested.

'Who's a pretty boy, then?' she asked.

'Pug is!' cheered Lady Miranda, patting Pug on the head.

How nice, thought Pug.

Wendy was ready to pounce, but the parrot was too quick and, with a wink, it pinched a teaspoon and flew out of the window.

'Rio!' came a shout from outside.
'Riiioooooo! Bad bird!'

'Who's that?' asked Lady Miranda.

'The hotel owner, Mr Gregory,' replied
Wendy. 'Rio must be the parrot's name.'
She shut the window.

'Will that be all, m'lady?'

'Yes, thank you, Wendy,' said Lady
Miranda, feeding Pug a piece of jam
tart.

Pug had never had such an exciting breakfast.

Half an hour later, Pug and Lady Miranda climbed into the sedan chair. At the ready were Running Footman Will and Running Footman Liam.

'To the seaside!' ordered Lady Miranda.

The seaside?! Pug hadn't realised they were so close the sea. This was terrible news, because Pug was afraid of water!

Pug worried as the Footmen made their way through the cobbled streets of Pebbly Bay and finally arrived at the beach. There they dropped the sedan chair and Lady Miranda scrambled out with Pug under her arm.

'This is going to be exciting!' she said happily to Pug, but all he could think about was the water. It looked very rough.

Lady Miranda was keen to show Pug all the things that made being at the beach so much fun.

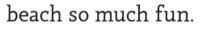

They started with a donkey ride, where Pug tried his best to steer away from the shoreline.

Then they built a sandcastle, until Pug had to be rescued as the water rose alarmingly in the moat.

Finally, Lady Miranda decided to bury Pug in the sand. She chose a quiet spot, close to Wendy. At first the sand tickled, but Pug soon became snug. Lady Miranda found him a sunshade and he settled down for a nap. Being on holiday was very tiring.

Nearby, a group of children was playing with a beach ball. They waved at Pug and Lady Miranda to join in their game. Lady Miranda began to dig Pug out, but Wendy suggested she leave him.

'He looks contented,' she said.

'*Woof!*' confirmed Pug.

'I won't be long,' Lady Miranda whispered in his ear. And off she went to introduce herself to the three children. The oldest boy was called Daniel, and the two girls were twins called Mimi and Hannah.

Unfortunately, as Pug couldn't catch, Lady Miranda hadn't had much practice. Daniel, Mimi and Hannah didn't seem to mind – they cheered whenever she *did* catch the ball, and chased after it whenever she accidentally threw it in the sea.

Pug's eyes grew heavy and he was about to doze off when a plane flew low over the beach. Behind it trailed a banner that read:

PEBBLY BAY PARADE TOMORROW

Distracted by the plane, Lady Miranda threw the beach ball wildly off course.

TOMORROW

She realised the danger almost immediately.

'Puuuuuuug!' she shouted in warning as it hurtled towards him.

But it was too late.

THUMP!

Lady Miranda was there in a second.

'Oh, Pug,' she wailed. 'Are you all right?'

Pug wasn't sure. Everything had gone blurry and he could see two Lady Mirandas!

'How many fingers am I holding up?' asked the two Lady Mirandas.

Pug, who was not very good at numbers, barked, '*Woof! Woof! Woof! Woof?!*'

Lady Miranda declared an emergency and sprang into action. She ordered Running Footman Will to make the sedan chair into a stretcher. Then she carefully laid Pug on it. Wendy packed up the picnic and parasol whilst Running Footman Liam emptied his shoes of sand in preparation for the run of his life.

The donkey lady handed them a helpful tourist map, which clearly marked the vet's. Lady Miranda squeezed Pug's paw and gave the order: 'Run!'

'Nee-naw! Nee-naw!' shouted Lady Miranda to make everybody get out of their way. And without too many wrong turns they soon found the vet's.

'He got a beach ball in his eye!' cried Lady Miranda as they rushed in with Pug.

Pug was whisked into the operating theatre. 'We'll take it from here,' said the vet.

Lady Miranda! thought Pug as his paw slipped from her hand.

Chapter 2

Lady Miranda, Running Footman Will, Running Footman Liam and Wendy looked at the patient.

Nobody knew what to say.

'He looks like …' began Wendy.

Pug hung his head. He felt silly wearing an eyepatch.

'Like a pirate!' said Lady Miranda.

'I was going to say panda,' said Wendy. 'A one-eyed panda.'

'Wait a minute,' Lady Miranda said, having one of her good ideas. She handed Pug to Running Footman Liam and popped into the Pebbly Bay gift shop.

Pug hoped they sold jam tarts, but Lady Miranda returned not with jam tarts but a pirate's hat.

'There!' she said triumphantly, placing it on Pug's head. 'Now he's a proper pirate.'

'Say, "aaaaaarh"', said Running
Footman Liam.

'*Grrrrrr.*' Pug tried his best.

'You'll get there,' said Lady Miranda
encouragingly.

Waiting for them outside the Smuggler's Rest were Daniel, Mimi and Hannah. Rio was perched next to them on the wall.

Running Footman Will and Running Footman Liam went off to turn the stretcher back into a sedan chair, and Wendy went to speak to the chef about the next day's menu.

'How's Pug?' asked Daniel when they'd gone.

'The vet said to give him some eye drops and to keep the patch on for a few days,' Lady Miranda replied. 'I've made him a pirate, so he doesn't feel silly,' she added.

Pug felt very silly indeed.

Just then three boys from the town walked by.

Daniel took a step back.

Mimi and Hannah pretended to look in the other direction.

Lady Miranda on the other hand smiled. 'Hello,' she said cheerily.

The boys sneered back. Then they saw Pug.

'Look at that stupid dog!' one snorted. 'He's dressed up like a pirate!'

The boys laughed so hard they bent double.

Lady Miranda held Pug closer and was about to say something very rude when Hannah stopped her.

'They're not worth it,' she whispered.

'Come on,' said Daniel. 'We have to meet our mum in the town square.

Do you want to come?'

Pug, Lady Miranda, Daniel, Mimi and Hannah headed off together, pleased to get away from the boys.

'Who are they?' asked Lady Miranda.

'Finnian, Caspar and Morgan,' replied Hannah. 'They're the meanest boys in town.'

Back outside the Smuggler's Rest, one of the mean boys had spotted Rio.

'There's that stupid bird!' said Finnian, picking up a nearby pebble. He thought everything was stupid.

'Get her!' cheered Morgan.

The three boys took aim at poor Rio, but, even before the first pebble was thrown, the parrot squawked in outrage and flew high in the air, out of reach.

Seeing her friends heading for the town square, Rio followed them.

The square was filled with banners and there were lots of dressed-up people milling about. They were getting ready for the parade rehearsal.

'Mum, this is Lady Miranda and Pirate Pug,' said Mimi.

'Hello,' said her mum.

Pug was surprised to meet someone else wearing a silly hat.

'I don't know if they've told you, but I'm the mayor of Pebbly Bay,' she explained.

'Pleased to meet you.' Lady Miranda did a little curtsy, and Pug barked.

'Every year the town celebrates the day it was freed from pirate rule,' said Daniel.

Pug felt embarrassed, seeing as he was now a pirate himself.

'Not pirates like Pirate Pug, here,' said the mayor. 'He's clearly a good pirate.'

Pug was relieved to hear it.

'About four hundred years ago, there was a really nasty pirate known as Finders Keepers,' Hannah informed them. 'He lived on the island in the middle of the bay and made every ship that passed by give him a share of its treasure.'

'He was very scary,' said Mimi.

'Then one day, Henry Hake, a local fisherman, gathered the people of Pebbly Bay, and together they drove Finders Keepers off his island. He was never seen or heard of again. Henry Hake became the town's first mayor.' Hannah pointed to his statue in the centre of the square.

Pug admired how smart the mayor looked.

'Show them your gold chain, Mum,' said Daniel.

'The people of Pebbly Bay paid for this to be made after they defeated Finders Keepers,' said the mayor, removing the chain from around her neck. 'It's a very important symbol for us.'

At that moment Rio flew down and landed on Lady Miranda's shoulder.

'She likes shiny things,' laughed Lady Miranda as Rio inspected the mayor's chain.

Just then, Finnian, Caspar and Morgan arrived in the square, armed with pebbles.

'There she is!' shouted Caspar, taking aim.

Spying them, Rio took flight, but she scooped up the mayor's gold chain as she took off.

'My chain!' shouted the mayor.

Rio rested for a moment on top of the statue of Henry Hake, struggling with the weight of the chain. But then she took off once more.

'Anyone who catches that bird and brings me back my chain can be mayor for a day!' the mayor proclaimed.

'After that bird!' shouted Finnian.

'The last thing we need is for Finnian to be mayor for a day!' said Daniel.

'Run!' shouted Lady Miranda as she gathered Pug in her arms and raced through the cobbled streets, following Rio back to the Smuggler's Rest.

As she sprinted through the doors of the hotel and out into the garden behind, she shouted, 'Mr Gregory, Rio has the mayor's chain!'

'Bad bird,' said Mr Gregory as they

both caught sight of her flying overhead. But instead of landing at the hotel, Rio carried on, over the sea, towards Finders Keepers' Island.

'You'd better get that chain,' said Mr Gregory grimly. 'Legend has it that if that chain is not worn by the mayor on parade day Finders Keepers will return to haunt the town.'

That didn't sound good to Pug, but then neither did the watery journey to Finders Keepers' Island.

Chapter 3

It seemed Pug wasn't going to be allowed to be one of those rare land-based pirates.

'Every pirate needs a ship, Pug,' Lady Miranda told him.

So Running Footman Will and Running Footman Liam carried Pug and Lady Miranda down to the harbour in the sedan chair. There they met Daniel, Mimi and Hannah.

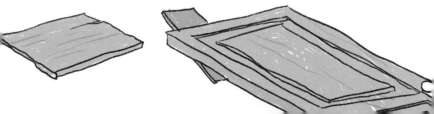

'We need to build a ship so we can get to Finders Keepers' Island,' Lady Miranda informed them. 'Mr Gregory has said we can use some old wood from the hotel.'

Lady Miranda negotiated with the donkey lady and borrowed two of her finest donkeys, Ella and Strawberry.

The new friends worked together to move the wood from the Smuggler's Rest down to the harbour. Once they'd assembled everything they set to work making a magnificent galleon.

Finnian, Caspar and Morgan

kept a watchful eye on them.

'Why aren't they building a ship?' asked Lady Miranda, hammer in hand.

'They're waiting for their dad to come back to harbour,' said Mimi. 'He has a really fast boat called the *Black Octopus*.'

Pug didn't like the sound of that one bit.

'We'll have to hurry,' said Lady Miranda.

Shipbuilding was hard work, but Pug did his best to help where he could.

Once they'd finished they had a small naming ceremony.

'I hereby name this ship *The Fearless*,' Lady Miranda proclaimed importantly.

WOOF!
WOOP!

The Fearless

The crew of *The Fearless*, including a very anxious Pug, climbed on board, unfurled the sails (which were some of Wendy's old aprons sewn together) and headed out to sea.

'To Finders Keepers' Island,' shouted Lady Miranda.

Daniel, being the eldest and the most experienced sailor, took the helm. Lady Miranda was on lookout.

'We can navigate by the stars,' she suggested, looking up at the clear blue sky through her telescope.

'It's daylight!' said Hannah.

'And the island's just there!' added Mimi.

The Fearless made surprisingly good progress out of the harbour.

Lady Miranda sat down next to

Pug, who was in charge of the ship's rations. Wendy had packed jam tarts for them all, to stave off scurvy. But in his nervous state Pug had already eaten half of them.

Lady Miranda patted him on the head and then handed round the remaining jam tarts. 'Wendy's finest,' she told the others.

'*Woof!*'

'You've had your share, Pug,' Lady Miranda admonished him.

'I think he was referring to that!' said Daniel.

A boat with a black sail was approaching on their port side.

'The *Black Octopus*,' said Lady Miranda in horror.

Chapter 4

Lady Miranda grabbed the telescope. Finnian, Caspar and Morgan were working hard. 'They're gaining on us!' she shouted miserably.

The crew of *The Fearless* started to panic.

'All hands on deck!' ordered Lady Miranda, rushing from starboard to port. (Or was it port to starboard?) All hands – and paws – were in fact already on deck, as there was nowhere else to go on *The Fearless*.

'Can't we go any faster?' shouted Lady Miranda.

In the confusion, Pug somehow ended up in charge of steering.

The *Black Octopus* was within shouting distance of *The Fearless*.

'Can I interest you in a jam tart?' Lady Miranda called out, trying to appease them.

'We want your boat!' Finnian yelled back.

'And a jam tart,' shouted Caspar.

Finnian hissed at him to 'shut it'.

Pug was trying his best to steer away from them, but he had got his left and right muddled up, which after numbers was his least favourite thing to learn. While he was considering the options, *The Fearless* was on a collision course with the *Black Octopus*.

'Not that way, Pug!' shouted Lady Miranda too late. *The Fearless* smashed into the side of the *Black Octopus*, sending both crews toppling.

Finnian regained his balance first.

'This means war!' he declared, boarding *The Fearless* and taking Pug prisoner.

Pug gave a nervous wag of his tail. He was very sorry about their boat. He hadn't meant to do it. It was an accident.

That meant nothing to Finnian who, now back on board the *Black Octopus*, held Pug aloft for them all to see.

'Everyone knows what happens to pirates who break the code,' he said.

Pug didn't even know there was a code. He thought Finnian was making it up.

'Poor little pirate dog is going for a walk,' laughed Morgan.

'Oh no!' said Hannah.

'Oh no, what?!' asked Lady Miranda.

'It's time to walk the plank,' Caspar informed them.

The crew of the *Black Octopus* strapped a plank to the side of their boat. It hung dangerously over the water.

Pug looked at the dark waves below.

He hoped there weren't any sharks.

'Please don't make him walk the plank,' pleaded Lady Miranda. 'He's just a pug.'

'I thought he was a pirate,' said Finnian.

'Yeah,' agreed Caspar. 'And as a pirate he has to accept a pirate's fate.'

Was it Pug's imagination or was the water getting closer?

He looked to Lady Miranda for reassurance.

'Don't worry, Pug! I'll rescue you!'

Finnian wobbled the plank, forcing Pug to shuffle closer to the edge. Bravely he turned to face his foe and mustered his best pirate's '*Grrrrrrr!*'.

As he growled, he realised his bottom was wet.

He looked behind him nervously.
The plank was now at water level.

'We're sinking!' wailed Morgan.

'You've sunk our ship!' Finnian accused Pug.

It was true. The collision had made a hole in the side of the *Black Octopus* and they were rapidly taking on water.

'Abandon ship!' shouted Lady Miranda.

Finnian, Caspar and Morgan hurriedly jumped on board *The Fearless*.

'I think you're forgetting something,' said Lady Miranda, dashing across the now sodden deck of the *Black Octopus* and rescuing Pug from the plank. He gave her a quick lick of gratitude. He knew she'd never leave him behind.

'It's your choice,' said Finnian to Daniel, Mimi and Hannah. 'Either you join our crew and act like real pirates or you sink beneath the waves with Lady Fancy Pants and her spoilt pooch ...'

'You're not real pirates,' said Daniel, stepping on board the disappearing *Black Octopus*. 'Real pirates don't borrow boats from their dad.'

'Or throw stones at birds,' said Hannah joining him.

'Or get their mums to tie their shoelaces,' added Mimi, following the others.

Morgan and Caspar both looked at Finnian, who blushed.

'*The Fearless* is ours now!' he jeered back. 'No matter what you say.'

He pushed *The Fearless* away from the doomed *Black Octopus* and the wind filled Wendy's wonderful apron sails.

'What are we going to do?' asked Hannah.

'Sink or swim, I suppose,' said Daniel.

Pug knew it would be sink for him. He looked at the water with great concern. It was already up to his tummy.

But Lady Miranda was not going to give up that easily. 'Quick – to the lifeboat,' she ordered. Being an excellent lookout, she'd spotted it earlier.

They hurriedly climbed in.

'How many souls on board, Pirate Pug?' Lady Miranda asked as they cast off.

'*Woof! Woof! Woof! Woof! Woof!*'

'Good work!' she patted him on the head.

For once Pug was glad to be on a boat. They drifted away from the *Black Octopus* as she bubbled under the waves.

'Finnian's dad's going to be really mad,' said Daniel.

The crew of *The Fearless* was cast adrift, but all was not lost.

'Grab an oar, Pug,' ordered Lady Miranda. 'We're heading for dry land.'

This was the best news Pug had heard all day.

Chapter 5

The crew of *The Fearless* made landfall at Stub Toe Cove on Finders Keepers' Island. The island felt almost tropical. There were lots of trees and lush undergrowth, and thankfully no sign of Finnian and his crew.

'We need to find Rio before the sun goes down,' said Lady Miranda. 'Let's split up.'

Pug looked concerned. He didn't like being separated from Lady Miranda.

'It's all right, Pirate Pug,' she said, comforting him. 'You stay here and guard the lifeboat.'

Lady Miranda and Daniel took the coastal path, over some sharp rocks.

Mimi headed towards the highest point on the island.

And Hannah followed a line of trees she thought would appeal to Rio.

Pug didn't much like being left alone so close to the sea. Plus he was beginning to feel hungry. He heard a strange sound.

Was that my tummy? he wondered as he heard the noise again.

'SQUAWK!'

Rio!

Pug bravely followed the noise into what seemed like a jungle.

Where would I go if I were Rio? he wondered. He liked the idea of being a bird, but worried that, with his large tummy, he'd find it difficult to take off.

As he pondered these things he came into a clearing with an old shack in the middle. Pieces of broken glass hung from string outside the door. They glinted in the sunlight.

This, Pug decided, *is exactly where Rio would be.*

Pug carefully nosed open the door. It creaked loudly, and sure enough Rio flew out of the shack.

'Who's a pretty boy, then?' squawked the parrot. (Pug did love Rio.)

Then he noticed something else.

There, on the floor of the shack, was the mayor's chain! Lady Miranda was going to be so pleased with him.

Pug picked it up and thought he'd try it on for size. He was just admiring his reflection when a shadow darkened the doorway.

'Not so fast,' said Finnian.

Pug shrank back. He desperately wanted Lady Miranda to be there. She'd know what to do.

'You don't want to be mayor for a day anyway, do you, Pirate Pug?' said Finnian, grabbing the mayor's chain from around Pug's neck and slamming the door of Finders Keepers' shack in his face.

'Quick, run to the boat!' shouted Finnian from the other side of the door. 'We've got it!'

Pug heard footsteps moving away from him followed by a desperate cry for help.

Pug tried the door, but it wouldn't budge. He pulled a chair towards a table by the window and jumped up.

Finnian, Caspar and Morgan were waist-deep in sand.

'It's quicksand! HELP!' shouted Finnian.

Pug could see they were in trouble. He took two steps back, closed his eyes and, like a true hero, ran at the glass.

Pug sailed through the air and landed, quite gracefully, on the porch. He rushed over to Finnian, Caspar and Morgan, while Rio flew off to get help.

Finnian was still holding one end of the mayor's chain, but the other end was on solid ground next to Pug's feet. Pug took hold of it in his mouth. Then Caspar grabbed hold of Finnian, and Morgan clung on to Caspar.

Pug started to pull.

'Keep going!' said Finnian, lifting up from the quicksand. 'You're doing brilliantly.'

'HELP!' shouted Morgan, who was sinking the fastest.

Then, to Pug's relief, Lady Miranda appeared. She clasped her hands around Pug's tummy and Daniel put his hands around her waist. Then

Mimi and Hannah arrived and joined in too.

They pulled like a tug-of-war team, heaving for all they were worth. But the crew of the *Black Octopus* was stuck fast.

Finally, Rio came to help too, and with a satisfying *POP!* Finnian, Caspar and Morgan were free.

Both crews collapsed in a heap, safely away from the danger.

The crew of the *Black Octopus* dusted the sand off, and Lady Miranda helped Finnian tie his shoelaces, which had come undone. Together they walked to *The Fearless*, which was moored in a small lagoon.

Before they boarded, Finnian handed Pug the mayor's chain. 'I think this is yours,' he said, placing the gold chain around Pug's neck. Everyone cheered.

'Any ideas how you're going to spend your day as mayor?' Lady Miranda asked Pug as she set their course for Pebbly Bay.

Pug had a think.

Chapter 6

The morning of the Pebbly Bay Parade had arrived. Because Pug was mayor for the day, the parade started from the Smuggler's Rest Hotel. The chef had made an extra-large batch of jam tarts, which Lady Miranda, Daniel, Mimi and Hannah handed out to the cheering crowds as Pug was lifted high on people's shoulders and carried through the streets.

Rio flew overhead squawking.

When they reached the square, Pug made a short speech …

'*Woof!*'

Which was greeted with rapturous applause.

He then gave out various prizes for the best fancy dress, the coconut-shy champion and the finalists in the fishing contest.

By mid-afternoon, his work was done and he was ready for a nap.

Everyone agreed that Pug had been an excellent mayor – clearly pirates weren't *all* bad after all.

Back at No. 10, The Crescent, Wendy was preparing a fish supper. Lady Miranda was giving Pug a bath, and Running Footman Will and Running Footman Liam were looking through their holiday snaps.

'Do you think it's a pirate's life for Pug, m'lady?' asked Wendy.

'I don't think so,' replied Lady Miranda, lifting Pug out of the bathtub and towelling him dry. 'He's too kind, Wendy. He'd always return the treasure, which I think is against the pirate's code.'

Lady Miranda and Pug sat down by the fire. 'Don't worry, Pug,' she whispered, giving him a hug, 'I won't ever make you a pirate again.'

Pug sighed with relief.

'I'll just have to think of something else you can be instead.'

THE BEST FISHERMEN

Laura James's love of storytelling began at an early age and led her to study Film and Writing for Young People at Bath Spa University. The adventures of Pug are based on the antics of her very own adventurous dogs, Brian and Florence. Laura lives in the West Country.

Églantine Ceulemans was born in Belgium where she spent her childhood devouring comics before moving to France to study illustration. As well as drawing, she loves riding her blue bicycle, cooking (which she is not very good at) and cleaning windows (which she is very good at). Églantine lives in Paris, France.